I0829496

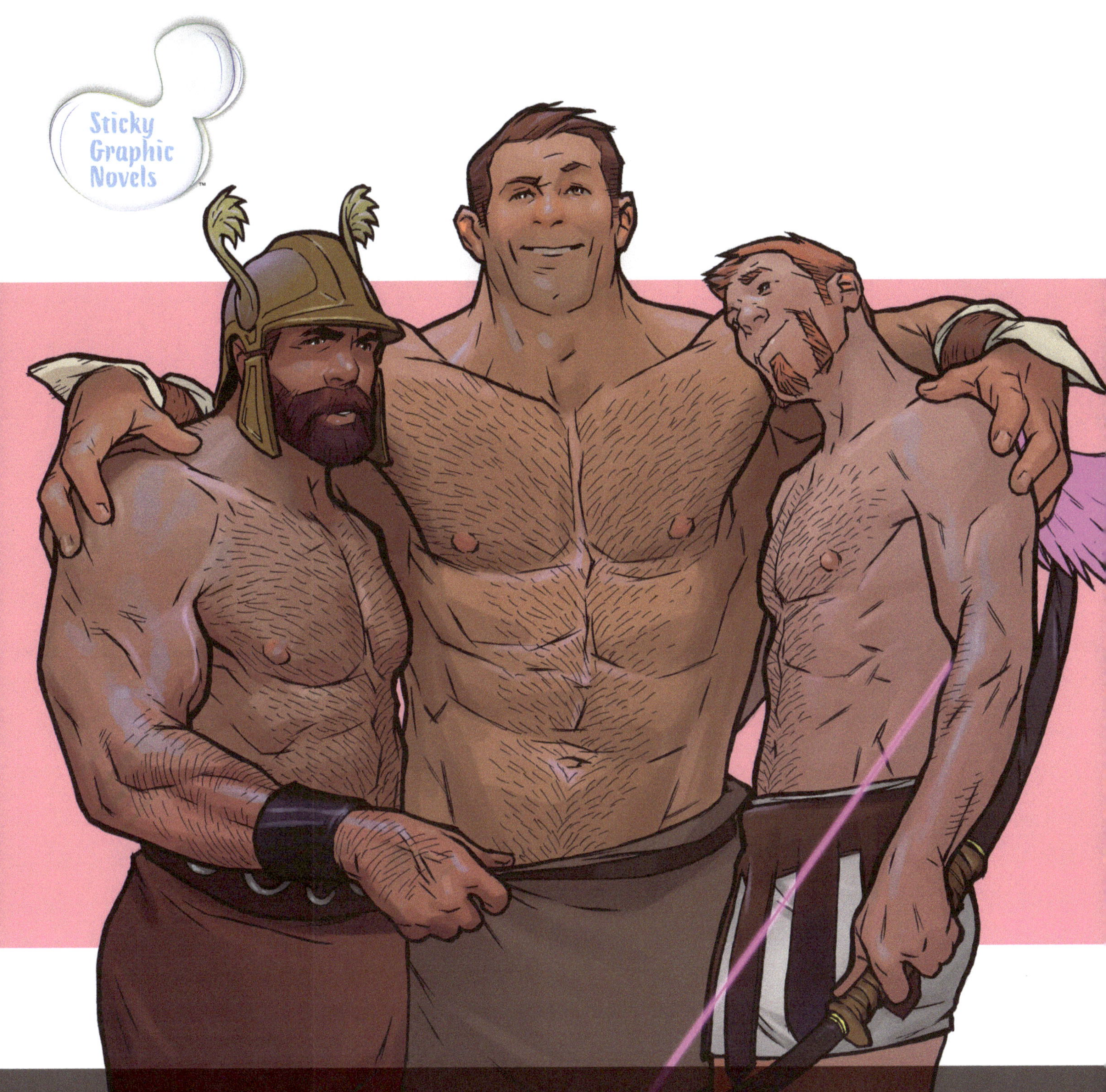

GREEK LOVE
— The Herculean Edition —
Dale Lazarov & Adam Graphite

GREEK LOVE
The Herculean Edition

Script and art direction by Dale Lazarov
Linework and colors by Adam Graphite
©2014 Dale Lazarov & Adam Graphite. All rights reserved.

StickyGraphicNovels.com

Printed and distributed by
ComicMix, LLC.
71 Hauxhurst Ave.
Weehawken, NJ 07086
http://www.comicmix.com

Printed in USA.

Hardcover ISBN: 978-1-939888-56-3

GREEK LOVE

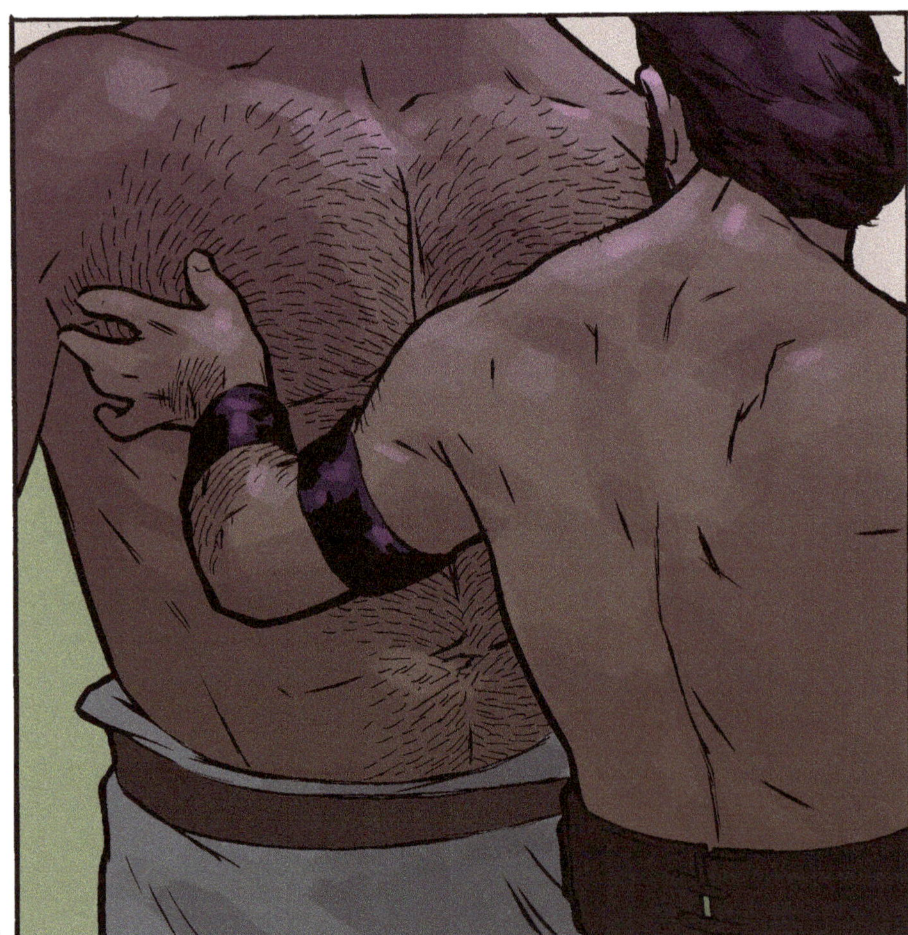

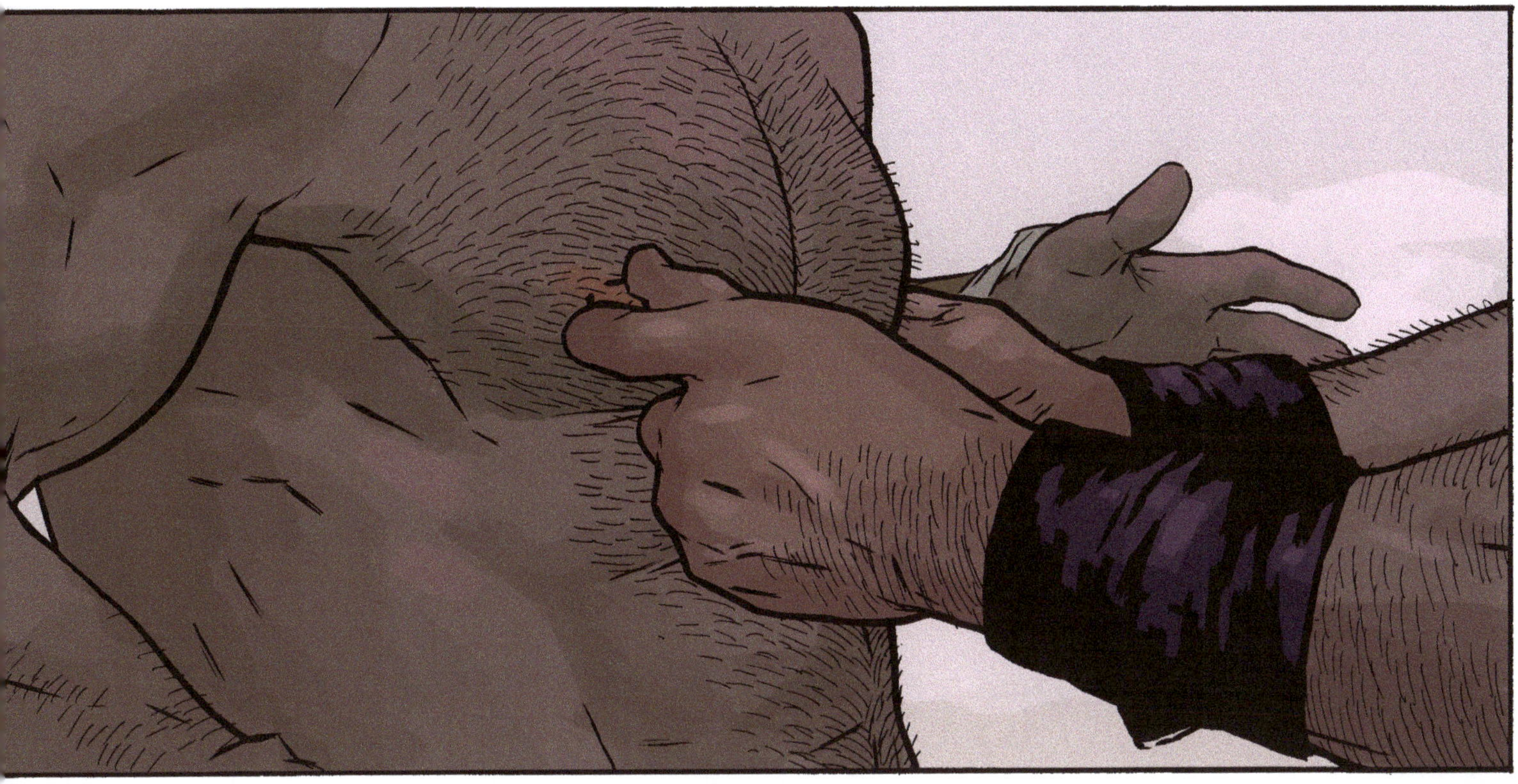

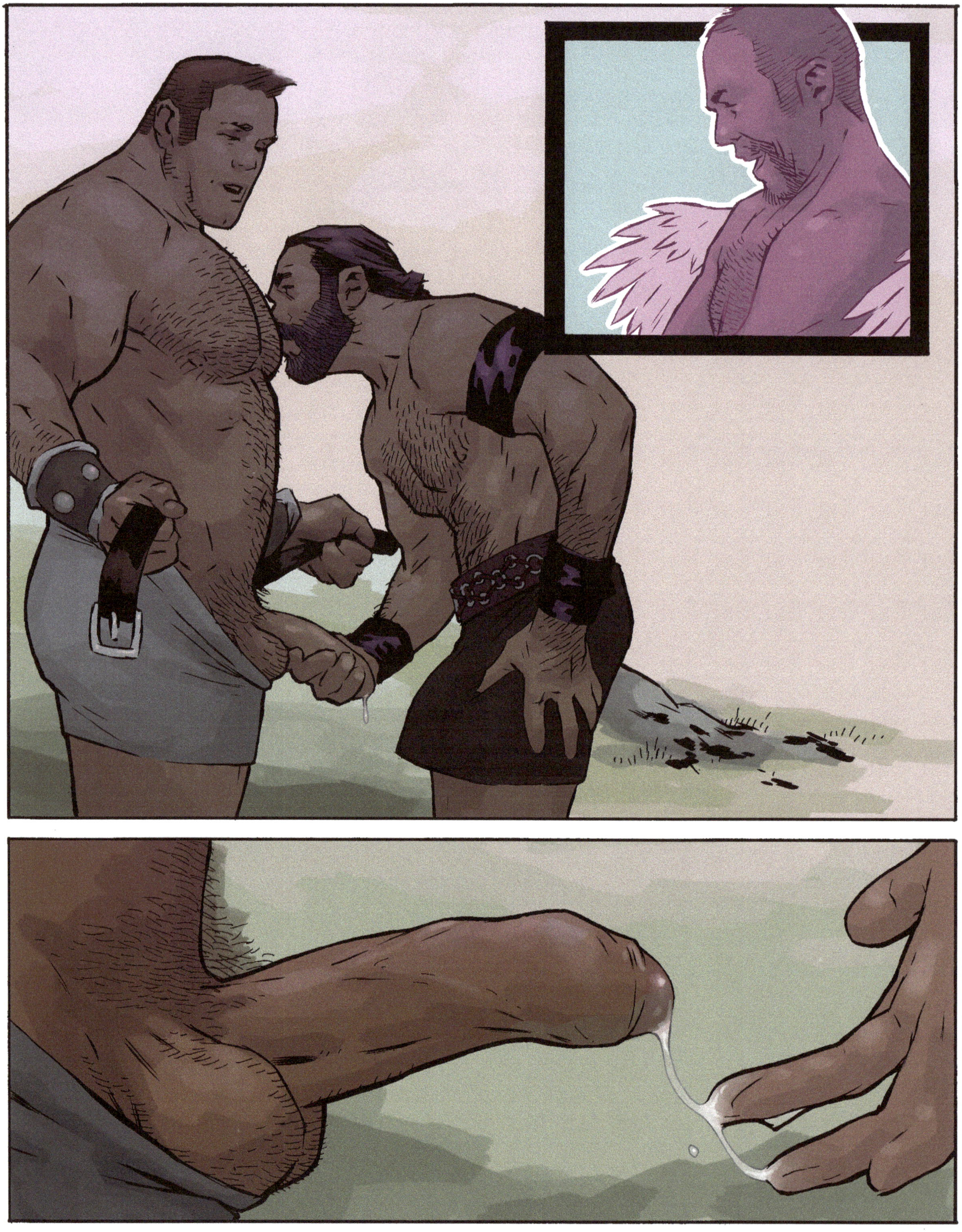

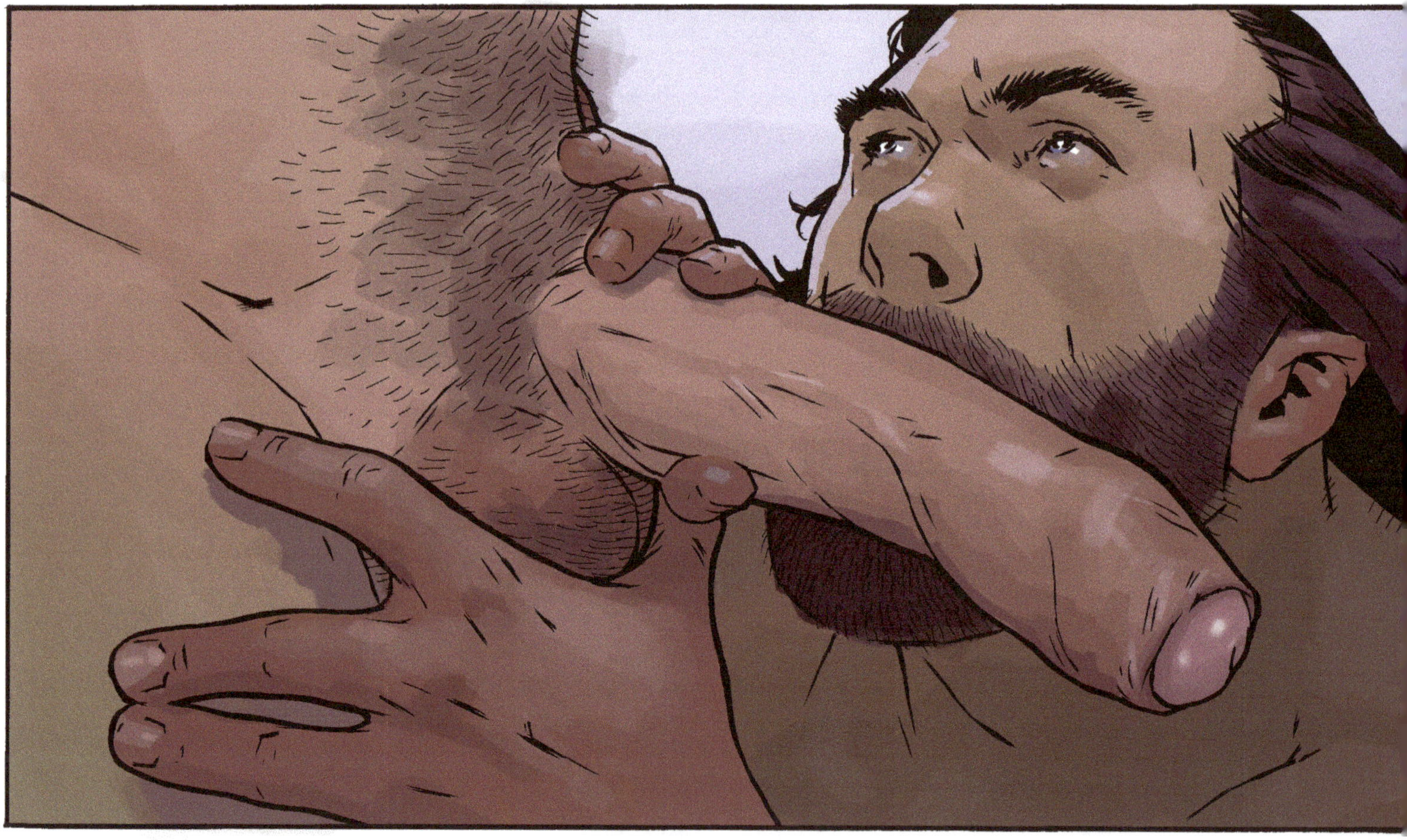

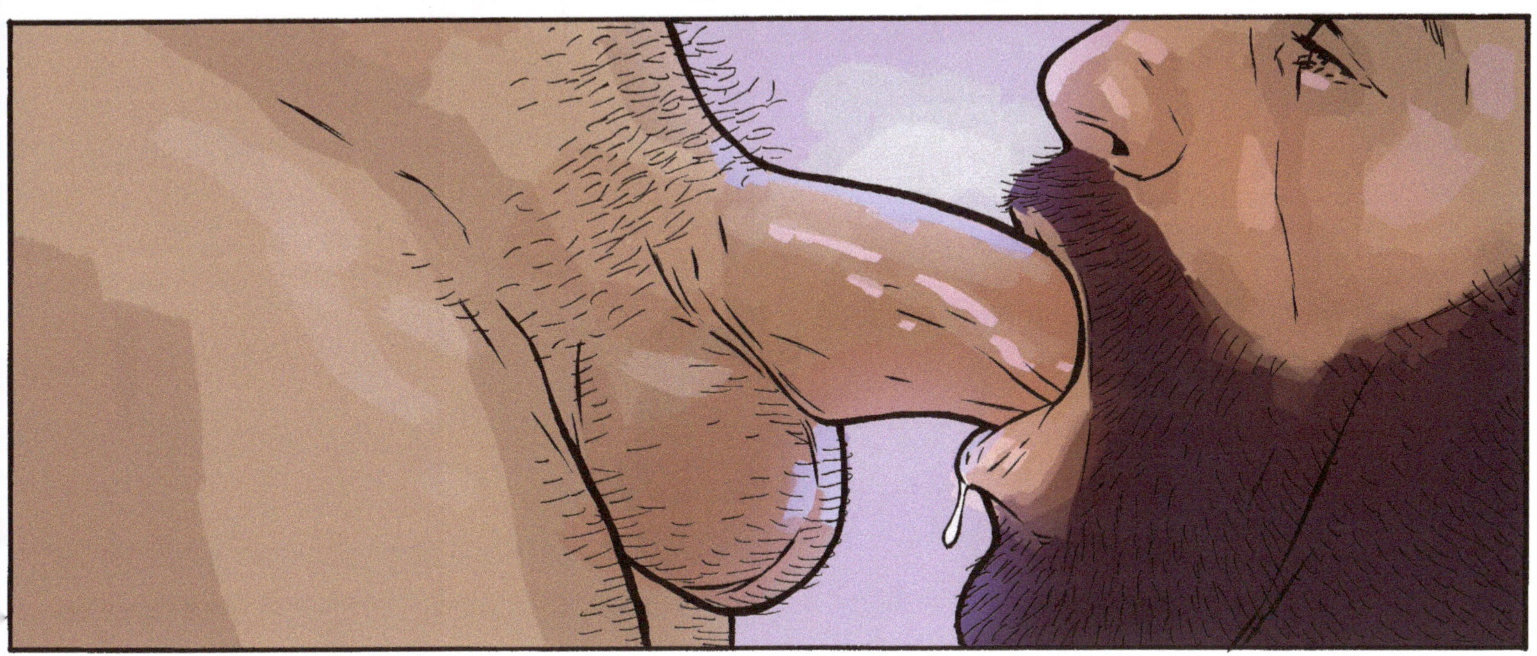

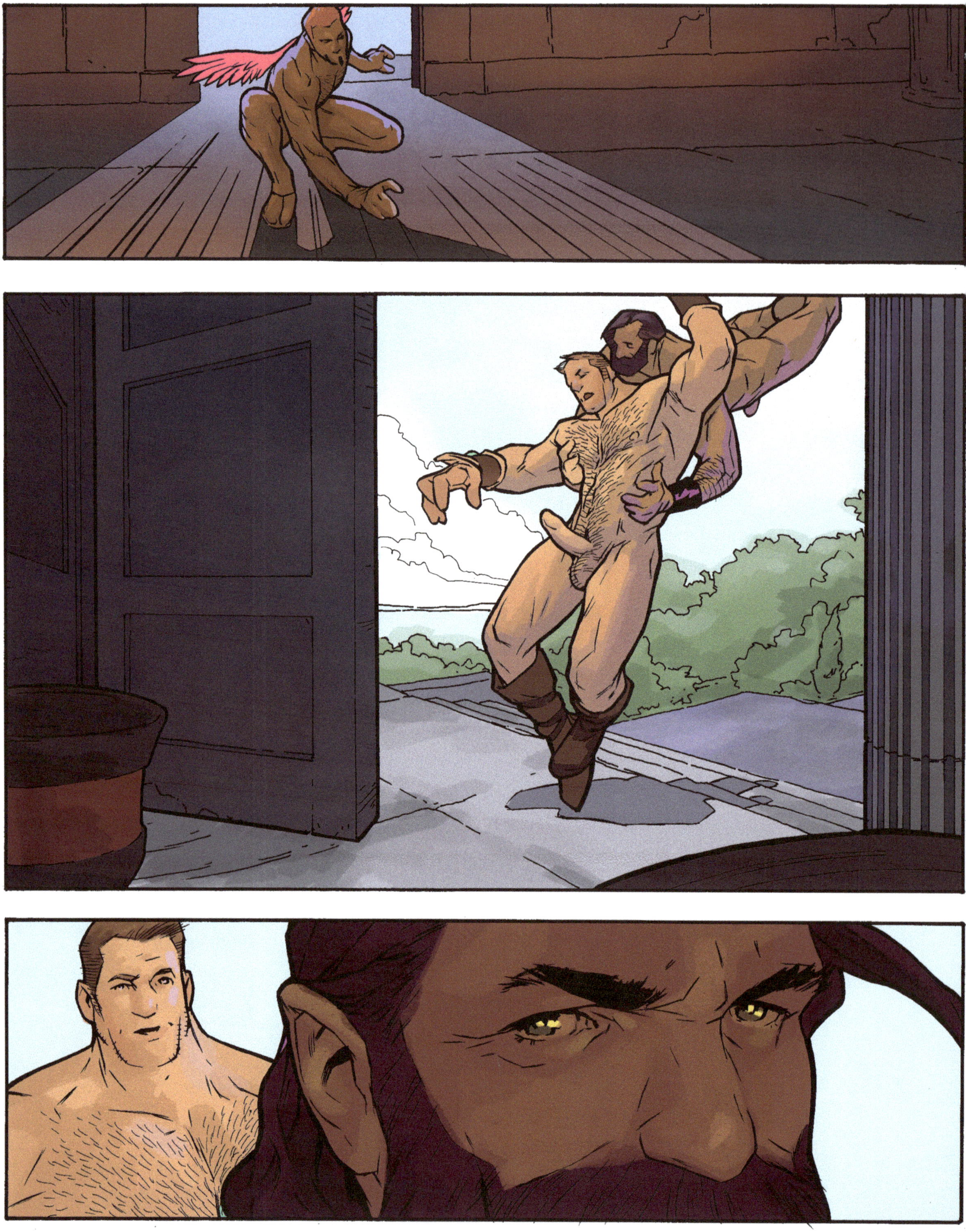

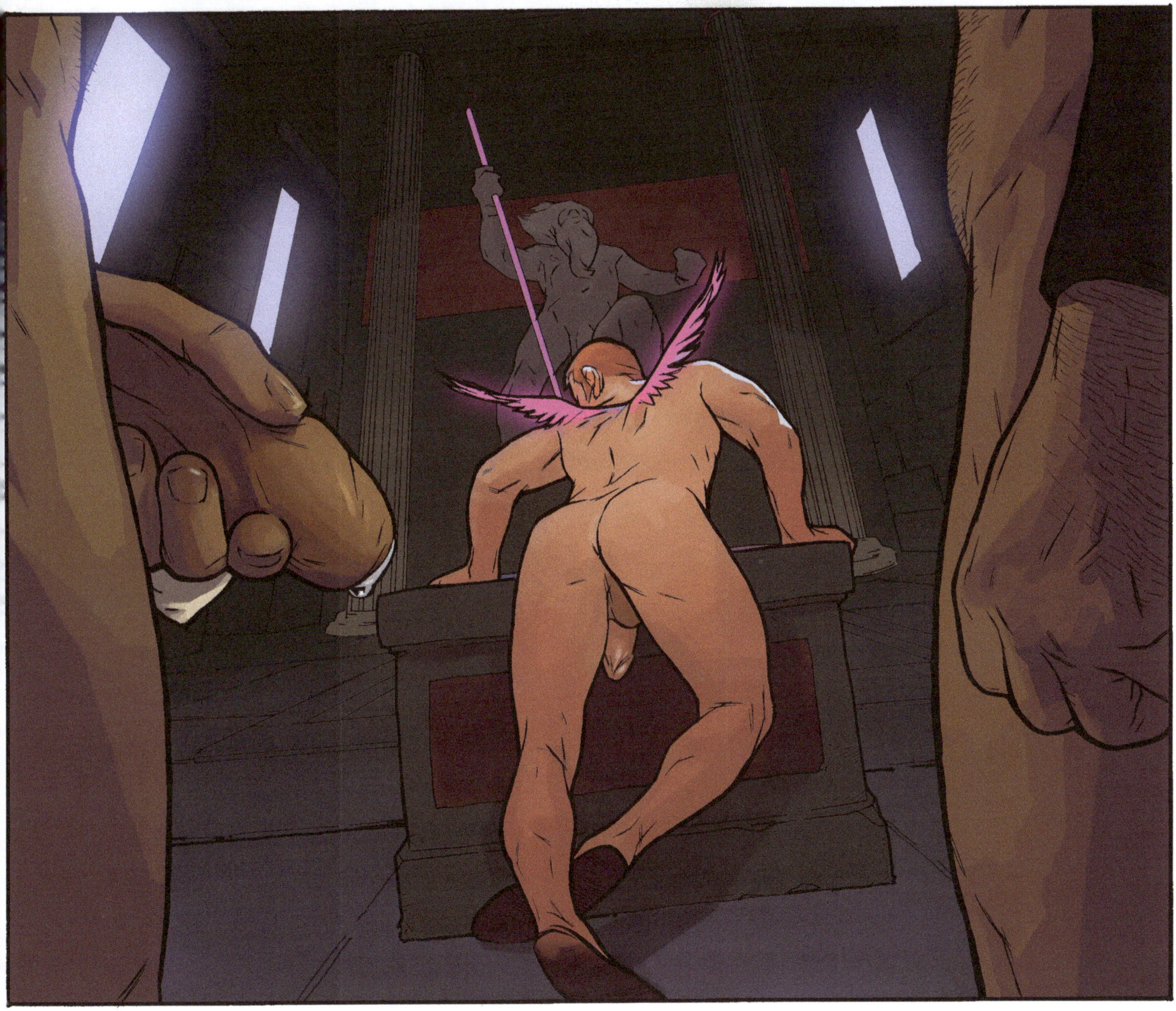

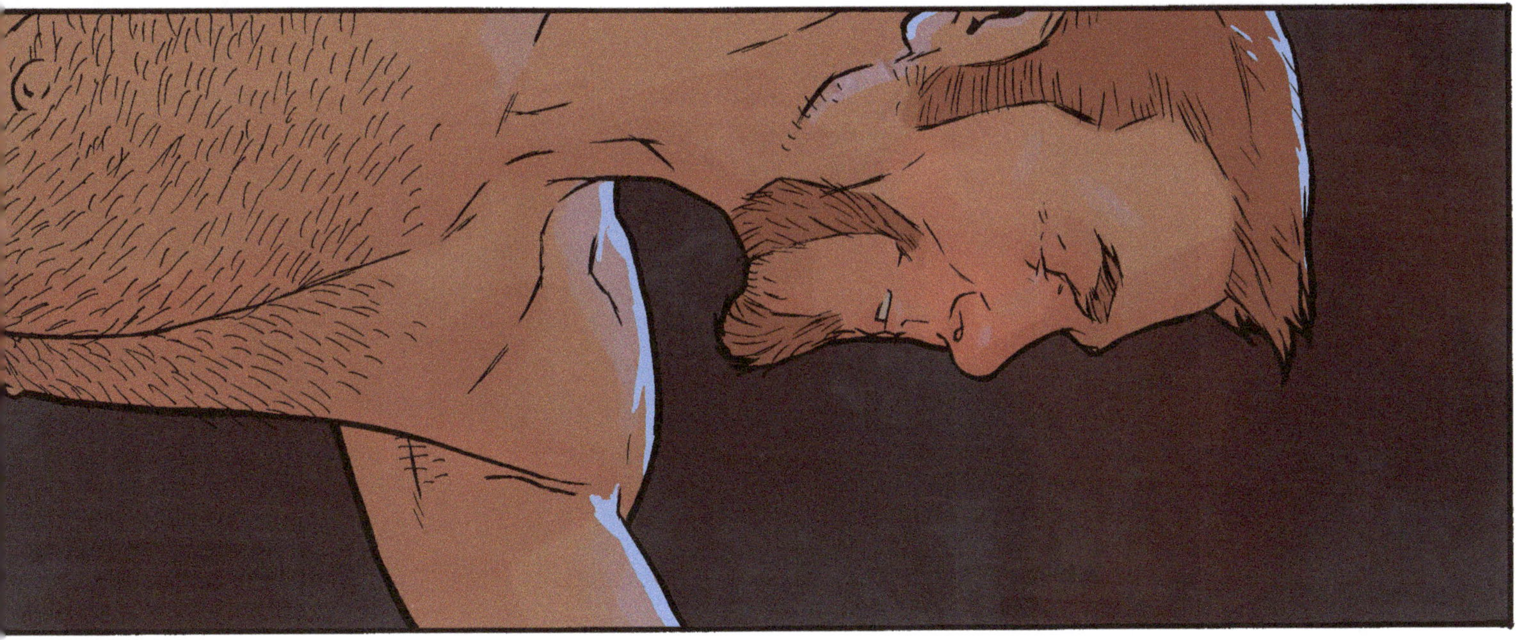

THE END

GREEK LOVE
THE HERCULEAN EDITION
script/edits: Dale Lazarov
art/colors: Adam Graphite

About The Authors:

<u>Dale Lazarov</u> is the writer/art director of CARNAL (drawn by theAmir), SLY (drawn by mpMann), BULLDOGS (drawn by Chas Hunter & Si Arden), PARDNERS (drawn by Bo Revel), PEACOCK PUNKS (drawn by Mauro Mariotti), FAST FRIENDS (drawn by Michael Broderick), GREEK LOVE (drawn by Adam Graphite), GOOD SPORTS (drawn by Alessio Slonimsky), NIGHTLIFE (drawn by Bastian Jonsson), MANLY (drawn by Amy Colburn), and STICKY (drawn by Steve MacIsaac) — wordless, gay character-based, sex-positive graphic novels published in hardcover by ComicMix and in digital format through Class Comics. He lives in Chicago.

<u>Adam Graphite</u> is a gay erotic artist who lives in Philadelphia, PA. This is his first published comic after years of drawing them for pure enjoyment. View his comics art at graphitestudio.tumblr.com and graphitestudio.deviantart.com.